The Horse in the Attic

The Horse in the Attic

By Eleanor Clymer

Illustrations by Ted Lewin

BRADBURY PRESS   SCARSDALE, NEW YORK

Bradbury Press, Inc.
2 Overhill Road
Scarsdale, N.Y. 10583
An affiliate of Macmillan, Inc.
Collier Macmillan Canada, Inc.
Manufactured in the United States of America
10 9 8 7 6 5 4 3 2 1
The text of this book is set in 12 pt. Palatino.
Library of Congress Cataloging in Publication Data
Clymer, Eleanor Lowenton.
The horse in the attic.
Summary: Twelve-year-old Caroline's discovery of a forgotten
painting in the family barn leads to her father's restoration
of the portrait of Sprite, a filly in the Racehorse Hall of
Fame, and a revelation about the previous owners of their old
house.
[1. Horses—Fiction.   2. Mystery and detective stories]
I. Lewin, Ted, ill.   II. Title.   ·
PZ7.C6272Hn   1983   [Fic]   83-6377
ISBN 0-02-719040-4

For F. R. D.

The Horse in the Attic

Chapter 1

This is a story about me and a horse. My name is Caroline Keating, and I love horses. It's also about my Dad, who loves horses too, but his interest is different from mine, as you will see.

I know people will say, "All girls are crazy over horses." Maybe so, and lots of boys like horses too.

Some girls (and boys too) grow up in families where they take horseback riding for granted. On a ranch, for instance, or a farm. Some get hooked on *Black Beauty* or *Misty* or *The Black Stallion*. Or maybe they were taken to the zoo when they were little and given a pony ride. That's how I got my start. It happened when I was about six.

We lived in the city. Me, Dad, Mother and my brother, Tom. He's four years older than I am.

Dad worked in an office, in some kind of insurance business. I had no idea what he did. He just went to work every day, came home, ate dinner and then he would read or play games with us, and go to bed. What a boring life! Grownups did terribly boring things. Mother too. She worked at home, typing manuscripts for people. She let me read some of them. I thought, "How can she stand typing other people's books? I'd rather write my own." Then she had the house to take care of—cleaning, shopping, laundry, cooking. I guess Tom and I took it all for granted.

On weekends, though, we did other things. We might all go to the beach, or have a hike and a cookout. And sometimes Dad would take us to the park so Mother could have some time off. I played with kids my age, and Tom played ball with his friends. Dad would sit on a bench and sketch.

He liked to sketch. He drew the children in the sandbox or on the swings, and he drew Tom playing baseball. He always had a pad and pencil with him. Tom and I were so used to it, we hardly noticed. Most parents had cameras to take pictures of their kids, but our Dad drew pictures.

Mother said he used to paint a lot when he was young. Some of his pictures were on the walls in our house. He wanted to be an artist, but he gave it up when he had a family to support. Except for sketching.

Well, one time he took me to the zoo. Tom and Mother had gone shopping or something. I remember that day because it was only me and Dad and something special happened.

Dad said to me, "How would you like a pony ride?"

We went over to the ring and he put me on a shaggy brown pony. I was a little scared at first, but the ponies walked slowly round and round in a ring of tanbark, their hooves going clop, clop, clop. A boy held me on so I wouldn't fall off, but in a few minutes I was sure I could stay on by myself. I held on to the saddle, and after a while I reached over and patted the pony's neck. It felt warm and rough. I patted harder, and a cloud of dust flew up.

When we stopped, I didn't want to get off, so Dad said I could go around again.

When we finally had to leave, I said to the pony, "Thank you for the ride." Everybody laughed. I didn't see why.

After that I begged for more pony rides. We went quite often, and Dad sat on a bench and sketched the ponies and the children. I still have a drawing he made of me on a pony.

But then I got too big for ponies, and we did other things. Sometimes Dad took me to museums or art galleries.

Some of the pictures we saw were beautiful—paintings of landscapes and ships and the ocean and so on. Others were weird—women with two eyes on the same side of their faces, or canvases covered with blobs of paint, or maybe just big expanses of one or two colors.

The ones I liked best were pictures of something happening, like people at a fair, or farmers gathering hay. It seemed the ones Dad liked best were of horses.

We looked at horses on farms, or in battles or with riders playing polo. We saw Chinese horses, fat and round, and horses on Greek vases, long and thin, and horses carrying knights in armor. We saw copies of paintings made on the walls of caves, by prehistoric people thirty thousand years ago, and English hunting scenes, with people in red coats riding to hounds, chasing a fox. There were fire horses and gypsy horses, and Indians on horseback hunting buffaloes.

Once, at the Metropolitan, we saw one of the horses of San Marco, a great gold sculpture that was sent here from Venice.

Dad looked for paintings by famous artists, like Stubbs, and Remington. He said Stubbs was the greatest painter of horses who ever lived. He was English. And Remington was a famous American painter. He painted western scenes, with horses and cowboys and Indians. He was a sculptor too.

We saw pictures of race horses. Dad made sketches of some of them. Once he actually took me to a race. He let me bet some money. (I lost.)

The races were so exciting, I jumped up and down and screamed. Dad just sat and sketched. He said racing was beautiful.

"Look at those muscles," he said. "Look at the way they move!"

I didn't understand then, but I do now. He was making a study of horses. He was specializing. And at the same time he was teaching me something about art.

However, what really sank into my head was that riding would be lots of fun. One day when we were walking home through the park, we came to the bridle path and waited while some riders went past.

I said, "I wish I could ride. It must be fun."

"Yes, it is," Dad said. "Maybe some day you'll learn. But not just now."

That night at dinner, I said, "Why can't I have riding lessons?"

"They're too expensive," Dad said, "especially in the city."

"How much do they cost?" I asked.

When he told me I was surprised. "Then let's go somewhere else," I said. "I wish I could learn. I wish I had a horse."

Mother said, "Caroline, don't talk nonsense." Then she said to Dad, "Don, why do you get her all excited about horses when we can't afford it?"

I felt bad for a while. But I didn't stop thinking about horses. I read books about them, and I started a collection of horses, china and plastic and wood. I had a stuffed one that I took to bed. And I would daydream about riding across fields on the back of a spirited horse.

Then, when I was eleven, something happened. We sublet our apartment and rented a house for the summer. It was in a village called Bridgeton and belonged to a man Dad knew through his job. He and Mother said it was cheaper than sending me and Tom to camp.

Dad commuted. He took the train to the city in the morning and came back about seven in the evening. He was hot and tired, but he said it was worth it to get out to where the air was fit to breathe.

The weekends and Dad's vacation were the best. Dad got an old car, and we would drive around and look at the scenery and take picnics, and Dad would sketch.

One day, we passed a field where some horses were grazing. They were beautiful—a silvery horse and a white mare with a little foal, and farther off some brown ones, standing under a tree and swishing their tails.

A little further on we came to a big barn, and a sign that said "Sunnyfield Stables."

"What's that?" I asked (as if I didn't know).

"It's a riding stable," Dad said.

"Can we stop and look?" I asked.

"Looking doesn't cost anything," said Dad. But it did.

We watched as some kids on horses came out and rode around the corral. Dad looked at me, and I looked at him.

He said, "Come on." We went inside and

asked how much riding lessons would cost. Then he said I could have some during the summer.

The lady in charge, Mrs. Harris, said I had to have a hard hat but I could wear jeans and shoes with heels. I wouldn't need boots.

Well, that was the best summer of my life so far. Dad drove me to the stables, and while I rode he would sit under a tree and sketch.

He drew me on my horse. I met a girl named Betsy Brownell and when she saw Dad's sketch of me, she wanted one too. She asked if she could take it home, and her mother framed it and hung it up.

Betsy's house was out beyond the village. Betsy had her own horse but she didn't have it at home. They kept it at the stable, and she groomed it every day and soon I was helping her. Mrs. Harris even let me help groom some of the other horses.

And Dad kept on with his drawing. Then one day he bought brushes and paints and canvases, and started painting.

Mother said, "I didn't know this was what you had in mind."

He laughed and said, "Neither did I."

Suddenly it seemed to me that Dad was happier than he had ever been. I mean, before, he always did what had to be done, and he was good-natured about it, didn't get mad or grouchy the way some grownups do. But he was never exactly happy or excited about anything. This summer, however, he really seemed to be enjoying life.

And we all were. We all had our own things to do. Mother played tennis, and Tom camped out with Kevin, a boy he met, and got jobs cutting grass and raking lawns. And Betsy and I went to each other's houses and read all the Misty books, and went swimming and of course riding.

But the summer came to an end. We had to go back to the city. We cleaned the house and packed our stuff and said good-bye and drove home.

Our apartment was stuffy from being closed up since the tenants left, and when we opened the windows the air was stale and the street noises were loud. And when I wanted to go outside I had to put on my shoes and go out in the hall and wait for the elevator, and then smell the gasoline fumes in the street. I thought, "Ugh! Who needs it? I wish I were back in the country."

Mother was cross. She said, "I need some

help unpacking and making the beds. And somebody has to go to the store and get something for dinner."

"Why can't Tom go?" I asked. But Tom had gone to see his friend Bob, who lived upstairs. Dad was out finding a parking place, and when he came back he grumbled.

The only good thing was that we had brought back tomatoes and corn and apples from the country, so we had something fit to eat.

Well, of course we adjusted ourselves. Dad went to work, Mother started to get our school clothes ready—we had to go shopping because we had grown so much. And after a while life went back to normal, the way it was before.

Living in the city was good in one way. I could go places on the bus or the subway and didn't have to wait to be driven in the car. Dad put the car in a garage. He talked about getting rid of it, but we said, "Oh, we may want it next summer."

And it was fall, and then winter, and Christmas. When they asked what I wanted for Christmas I said riding lessons. But they were too expensive in the city. I could have two or three, but I thought that would be worse than none, so I had none. I told myself that some day my chance would come.

Then it was February, and winter vacation, and I sat looking out of the window and thinking, "If we lived in the country I could go riding." It was one of those warm sunny days that suddenly turn up in the winter. It was a Saturday.

"I wish we were out in the country," I said.

Dad heard me. He had been reading the paper and drinking coffee.

"Let's go," he said, putting down his mug.

"Where to?" Mother asked.

"Oh, just for a drive," he said. "Who wants to come?"

Tom and Mother and I all had things to do. Tom had tickets to a basketball game at Madison Square Garden. Mother had a date to go to a matinee with a friend. I was going shopping with my friends, but I thought, "Who wants to shop?"

I phoned my friends and said I had to go someplace with my father, and Dad went to get the car. Mother packed a lunch for us.

"Where shall we go?" Dad asked.

"How about Bridgeton?" I said, and Dad said all right.

I had only been kidding and asked, "Isn't it too far?"

"Not really," Dad said. "Just a couple of hours' drive."

We drove along the parkway. There was snow on the fields, though the roads were dry and clear. It had snowed a couple of weeks before. Of course in the city it was all gone by then except for some dirty heaps with beer cans stuck in them.

"What will we do when we get there?" I asked, thinking it would be time to turn around and go home again.

Dad smiled and began to sing, which meant he was feeling good. I sang too, and before long we turned off the parkway into the two-lane road that led to Bridgeton.

Dad stopped the car at a wide place in the road and we got out. I sniffed the snowy air. It felt the way ice cream tastes, cold and clean. And it was so quiet!

We got back in the car and ate our lunch, and then we went on to Bridgeton.

"Hey, Dad," I said, "can I phone Betsy?"

"Sure," said Dad. "See if she's home."

We stopped in a diner and I phoned. Mrs. Brownell answered. When she heard we were in Bridgeton she said we must come over.

Betsy was riding but she would be home in half an hour.

We drove to their house. It was outside of the village, a big house on a hill, with acres of lawn and trees, all covered with snow.

I said to Dad, "Wouldn't it be nice if we lived in a place like that?"

He said, "I suppose so. I'd even be satisfied with something smaller."

When Betsy got home and saw me she screamed, "Caroline! How did you get here?"

We rushed into each other's arms.

Mrs. Brownell asked if we had had lunch. When we said yes, she said that we must stay for dinner.

Dad said no, we had just dropped in and we must start home right away. Then we looked out and it was snowing!

"Hey, what happened?" I asked. "It was a nice spring day."

"It doesn't look like a bad storm," Mr. Brownell said.

"I don't have snow tires," Dad said. "We'd better start right now."

"I have a better idea," Mrs. Brownell said. "Why don't you stay overnight?"

We said we couldn't. We hadn't meant to

come at all. But Mrs. Brownell said she would lend us pajamas, and we called Mother and stayed. We had dinner, and sat in front of the fire and played Scrabble, and then Betsy and I went to her room while the grownups talked, and finally we went to bed.

It was so quiet! And outside, everything was pitch-black except for the white fields and the snow falling so softly in the light from the downstairs windows.

When we woke up next morning everything was covered with a fresh coat of snow— the barn and all the trees. Every branch and twig was black, outlined in white.

Downstairs, Dad was in front of the big window sketching the snow-covered trees.

I wondered how we would get home, but he didn't seem worried. At breakfast, in front of the fire, I said, "I wish we lived out here. Hey, Dad, why don't you find us a house and we'll stay."

I thought he would tell me not to be ridiculous, but he didn't.

He said, "Okay, Caroline, if you say so."

And what do you think happened then? Mr. Brownell phoned a friend of his who was a real estate agent. Then he and Dad got in Mr.

Brownell's car, which was a Scout with four-wheel drive, and left. They were gone for hours.

Meanwhile Betsy and I went out and made a snowman, and threw snowballs at each other, and made angels, which you do by lying down in the snow and flapping your arms up and down.

At last the men came back. Dad said, "Well, that was quite an experience."

They had seen a few houses, which were all big and expensive. Then Dad had asked if there was anything smaller and more modest, and in the village because Mother didn't know how to drive. The man showed them an old brown-shingled house which he said needed work. When they say a house needs work, it means it looks as if it's about to fall down.

This house had been empty for a while. Dad made some sketches of it and said he would talk to his wife.

"And now," he said, "I think we had better start." Then he looked out at the road covered with snow and shook his head.

Mrs. Brownell had an idea. She was just full of ideas.

"Leave your car here and take the train," she said. "There's a train in half an hour."

So that's what we did. Mr. Brownell and Betsy drove us to the train. That train ride was the most exciting trip I had ever made. All the way in, Dad and I talked about the house. He showed me his sketches and drew a floor plan of the inside, and a map of the streets. The house had three bedrooms, a small yard in front, and a big yard in back with a garage or a shed or something that had once been a stable, long ago before people had cars.

"A stable!" I said. "Then maybe I can have a horse."

"One thing at a time," said Dad.

"What will Mother say?"

"A lot depends on that," he said.

Chapter 2

You can imagine Mother's reaction when she heard.

"Buy a house!" she screamed. "Don, are you out of your mind?"

Dad laughed happily and said, "No, I don't think so. Wait till you see it. It's not very fancy."

He showed her his drawings and told her what a nice garden she could have, and what good schools the village had, and how Tom would be on the football team, which he couldn't do in the city. And before we went to bed, he had her almost convinced that maybe we could swing it—that is, if she liked the house.

The following week, when the snow had melted, we all went to Bridgeton on the train.

Our first look at the house was a little discouraging. It was winter, and everything was pretty drab, with puddles of melting snow and mud in the yard, and water dripping off the roof. But Dad pointed out the wooden lace trim on the porch, and the carved railing. Inside, it was cold and damp, and the paint and wallpaper were peeling. But the rooms were nice and open, there was a bay window, and the stairway had a big wooden post at the corner.

We went out and looked at the stable and Tom said, "We can have a workbench here and make things."

"But where will we keep the car?" Mother asked.

"That will have to stay outside," said Tom. "This is too good to keep a car in."

The Brownells came to encourage us. They brought a carpenter along.

Mrs. Brownell told Mother all the plants she would give her from her garden. "And look at that big lilac bush," she said. "You'll love it."

"You can keep a horse in the stable," Betsy said.

"No, I can't," I said. "Tom wants it for a workshop."

"Well, anyhow, it will bring you good luck," she predicted. "Look at the horseshoe nailed over the door."

Sure enough there was one, upside down.

"What does it mean?" I asked.

She told us a story about some saint, St. Dunstan, I think, who was a blacksmith, and one night the devil came to his forge and wanted to have one of his shoes fixed. So St. Dunstan said he would do it, and the devil put his foot on the anvil, and when St. Dunstan got him there he tied him down and wouldn't let him go until the devil promised him something. He had to swear not to make trouble for a house with a horseshoe nailed over the door. The devil had to agree but he said the shoe had to be upside down.

"What a story!" I said. "Where did you get it?"

"Oh, I read it in some book," she said. "See if it comes true."

Meanwhile Dad and Mr. Brownell and the carpenter went all over the place and made a list of things to be done. There were a lot of them. We would need a new furnace, and storm sashes and new wiring, things you don't think of in the city. And some time we would need a new kitchen floor and cabinets.

The carpenter said the house was well built. It was one of the oldest in the village. He said the plumbing was all right too.

"Bob Ringo used to live here," he said. "He was a pretty good plumber. And he put in a new septic field just before he moved."

I didn't even know what that was. It seems it's what you have in the country when you don't have sewers.

Of course the house needed paint, but we could do that ourselves. Tom said he and his friend Kevin would do it free.

Mother and Dad decided to go home and think about it. The Brownells drove us to their place to get our car, and then the car wouldn't start. We had to take the train back to the city. The fare for four people both ways was pretty high, you better believe.

"We may have to get another car," Dad said. "That one is about shot. And you'll have to learn to drive," he told Mother.

"Me drive!" she exclaimed. "Well, why not? I'll have to get a job to help pay for all this, so I'll have to drive."

That night Mother and Dad talked and talked, and did a lot of figuring. At last they decided that if they could get a mortgage, they would buy the house.

The next week we went back to Bridgeton to see some lawyers, and a man at the bank, and Mother and Dad signed a contract to purchase the property consisting of house, land, outbuildings and contents. That made it sound like an estate, which it wasn't. Now all we had to do was pay for it, fix it up, and move in.

Well, I won't bore you with the details, because that isn't what this story is about. Weekends we worked on the house. We turned on the heat and slept on cots. We painted the inside to be ready for the furniture.

In April, daffodils and crocuses began coming up. In May there were tulips. And lilacs. The old dead-looking bush was covered with heavenly smelling purple flowers. The forsythia was a mass of yellow bloom.

Neighbors came to welcome us, bringing cakes. "What nice people!" Mother said. "In the city you hardly know your neighbors."

They offered to lend us things, but Dad said he'd have to buy his own. We needed a lawn mower, garden tools, a ladder, a hose and some buckets. There were lots of ways to spend money that we hadn't counted on.

At last we were ready to move. I said goodbye to my friends, and Mother told all her friends they must come out and see us. We packed our things, and the movers took the furniture and boxes away, and we got in the used station wagon Dad had bought, and were off.

What a thrill it was when we pulled up in front of the house! We climbed out of the car and stood and gloated. It was ours! Of course we were all happy, but I glanced at Dad, and on his face was a look of pure joy, as if he'd finally gotten what he wanted for Christmas.

There were two geraniums on the porch, and in the kitchen one of the neighbors had left a casserole.

We started unloading the car.

Mother said, "An empty house is nice. It's so uncluttered."

But then the moving men arrived and it wasn't uncluttered any more. From then on we worked like mad.

We moved furniture, unpacked dishes and books, put away clothes. Dad and Tom put up shelves and built a closet. They fixed up the workshop in the stable.

Dad was taking the first two weeks of July as his vacation, to get the house in shape. He fixed some windows and built a new cellar door. He was busy every minute.

Tom and Kevin and I started painting the trim on the outside. The boys did the high places, and I did the porch railings. That was fun.

Then we started on the garden.

Mother hadn't gardened since she was a kid, but she remembered a lot. She knew some of the plants that were coming up, and our neighbor Mrs. Dawson came over and showed her a lot more, and gave us some perennials from her garden. We had put in some tomatoes and lettuce and beans back in May, and they were doing fine. Mother was very excited about the garden.

Then she started to take driving lessons. Every day she came home bursting with excitement.

"Why didn't I do this before?" she kept saying.

I was waiting for the time to come when I could start riding lessons, but we were so busy I didn't like to mention it. Finally I suggested, "I could go with Betsy."

But Mother said, "It is rather expensive, dear. Maybe you'd better wait a while. Dad has a lot on his mind."

Dad really did seem to have a lot on his mind, mainly expenses. The heating man said we had to get a new furnace right away. And then the refrigerator stopped working. They said it wasn't worth fixing and we had better look for another one. Maybe a used one.

Mrs. Dawson said, "Why don't you look in the *Cent-saver?*" That was a little newspaper where people advertised things to buy or sell. Mother looked and found a refrigerator quite cheap. Then Mrs. Dawson advised us to go to tag sales.

That was real fun. Mother practiced her driving, and we found stuff for the house. I got a bookcase for two dollars, and Dad bought me a bicycle so I could get around the village on my own.

In almost no time, Dad's two weeks were over, and he said, "Well, tomorrow it's back to the salt mines."

"But Dad," I said, "your whole vacation went by and you didn't do any sketching."

"Oh, well," he said, "there's plenty of time. I'll have weekends, and after all we're staying here now. We don't have to get back to the city."

But *he* had to go to the city, coming home hot and tired, with things on his mind.

Then I realized that this summer wasn't like the summer before at all.

Tom didn't fool around and play ball. He and his friend Kevin were doing house painting. Kevin had a beat-up old truck and they drove around with their paint cans and ladders and got jobs.

Mother didn't play tennis. She found a job in a flower shop. She discovered she was crazy about plants and took a summer botany course on Saturdays.

And I wasn't taking riding lessons. When I wasn't hanging out with Betsy, I was vacuuming the house or getting supper started or baby-sitting. Mrs. Dawson had two little kids and was happy to have me mind them while *she* played tennis.

Oh, of course I did have *some* fun. I rode my bike up to Betsy's house and we swam in her pool, and played tennis on her court, and she came to our house and helped me arrange my model horses on my new bookcase. It was great to have room for all of them.

But then Mr. Brownell had to go to Europe on business, and he was taking Mrs. Brownell and Betsy along. I was devastated.

"What'll I do while you're gone?" I wailed.

"It's only for a week," Betsy said. "Till the first of August. I wish I didn't have to go but they think it will be educational for me."

So Betsy left, and I felt pretty sorry for myself. To make matters worse, they started putting in the new furnace. What a mess! The old one had to be dragged out through the cellar door, and the new one dragged in, and ducts and pipes installed. The whole place seemed to be torn up.

I didn't want to stay around the house alone. I rode my bike around the streets, went to the library, baby-sat, and sometimes I went over to the flower shop where Mother was in seventh heaven, making flower arrangements in fancy pots.

"I haven't got much to do," I complained.

"Oh," she said, "I hear there's a swimming class you might get into. Now here's some lovely cheese and fruit I just bought at the Village Market. Why don't you go home and make a snack and I'll be there about four. Then I'll phone about the swimming."

I didn't want a swimming class. I wanted riding lessons. But I knew I couldn't have them just yet. So I went home and fixed some lunch and went out in the garden to eat it. I couldn't stay in the house with all the uproar the workmen were making. It was boiling outside.

The door to the workshop was open. I went

in. At least it would be shady in there. I sat down on a box in the middle of the floor to eat my sandwich.

As I ate, I looked around. Tools were hanging on the walls. Cans of nails and screws were lined up on shelves. Paint cans were on the floor and brushes hung on a wire. Tom was very neat. I thought of the horse that probably lived in this stable long ago, and how surprised he would be to see his house full of tools. I wished the stable were bigger so I could have some space in it too.

As I looked around, an idea came to me. I went outside and looked at the building. I was right. It had a peaked roof, and a window at each end. But inside, there was just a ceiling. Wasn't there an attic under the roof? And if there was, how did you get into it? There was no stairway on the outside, and there was no way from the inside.

I climbed up on the box to get a better look at the ceiling. It was just rough boards. But at one end there was a place that looked as if the boards had been cut. Maybe that was a way to get up there. A trap door?

I found a stepladder and stood it under the cut place (if that was what it was). I climbed up and pushed at the boards. They didn't

move. I pushed harder. I went down and got a hammer and banged with all my might. Suddenly the thing flew open. It *was* a trap door. A square piece had been cut out of the ceiling and put back.

I climbed to the top of the ladder and poked my head inside. It was pitch dark and very dusty. I sneezed. Then I got down and found a flashlight and climbed up again.

Now I could see.

Chapter 3

It was an attic, all right. It was hot and dark and smelled of ancient dust. There seemed to be a lot of junk: broken chairs, a baby's high chair, some ancient wooden boxes. I crawled over to them and pulled open a couple. They were full of old books, with tiny print and dull green covers.

It was a big attic. The roof sloped down to the floor at the sides, but in the middle it was high enough to stand up in. I wished I had more light. Then I saw that the windows at each end were covered with wooden shutters. The shutters were held in place by some fasteners that you could turn, so I took them off. That was better. There was quite a good light then. It was terribly hot, but I thought that if I could get the windows open and bring a fan up, it wouldn't be so bad.

I explored some more. Against a wall I

found a stack of old pictures. I pulled them out and stood them up. Some were in gold frames, some in plain wood. One was a picture of a big old dog, another was a lady in a funny old-fashioned dress, with a tiny waist and a big bosom. There was a moonlight scene with boats on a river. And way at the back was a huge one. When I managed to drag it out, I saw that it was a painting of a horse.

It was scratched and covered with dust and the carved gold frame was chipped. There was a hole in one corner of the canvas. I pulled out the tail of my shirt and wiped some of the dust off the painting so I could see it better. It was a race horse, with a jockey on its back. The horse was black, with slender legs and an elegant head. Even dirty and scratched as it was, the painting looked beautiful.

I turned it over. On the back there was some writing. It said, "Sprite. O'Brien up. 1905."

Obviously Sprite was the horse and O'Brien the jockey. I couldn't see the name of the artist.

I wanted to take the painting down, and dragged it over to the hole, but it was too big to go through. So I stood it up again and looked at it. I wondered if it could have been a real horse. If only Betsy were home. I could hardly bear to wait till she got back.

But I had plenty to do. First I had to clean the place up. I got rags and a broom and dustpan and swept up piles of dust. I managed to get a window open, so I had some air. Then I had to clean myself up. I was filthy. I went to take a shower, leaving the trap door open so air could circulate.

By then Mother and Tom were home.

"What were you doing in the shop?" Tom wanted to know.

"I discovered an attic," I said. "Did you know it was there?"

"Sure," Tom said. "I had a heck of a time getting it open. It was nailed shut. I thought when I have time I'll take a better look."

I said, "Well, can I have it for my own workshop, since you've taken over the lower part?"

"Okay by me," he said. "But you'd better not use the stepladder. I'll put the big ladder up. It will be steadier."

"What's up there?" Mother asked.

"Just a lot of dust and junk," I said. "I cleaned it up a little."

I was glad they didn't ask any more ques-

tions. They were too busy with their own affairs, and I wanted this to be my private thing.

I went up every day and looked at the picture. I decided Sprite must be a filly, and I pretended she was mine, and was winning races and I was paying off the mortgage and restoring the family fortunes.

Then I went to the library and found books about horses. There was one book with a whole chapter about thoroughbreds. It said they were all descended from three breeds. I decided Sprite must be an Arab, and I would write a story about her.

I said to myself, "If I can't win races to restore the family fortunes, I can write stories."

I got a notebook and a pencil and started to write. This is how it went.

Once there was a girl who knew a lot about horses, having been raised on a ranch. She came east to visit her aunt, and one day as she was out walking, she saw this old peddler driving a horse and wagon, and beating the horse to make it go faster. The horse just stood there with its head hanging down, its bones sticking out, showing it had not been fed properly.

Suddenly the noon whistle blew.

The horse lifted its head and started to run. It took off down the street, the old man hanging on to the reins and yelling to it to stop.

The girl stepped out in the street and called out, "Stop!" When the horse heard her voice it stopped and looked at her.

"That is a good horse," the girl thought. "I wish I could buy her." She looked in her pocketbook and found a check her father had given her in case of emergency.

"Well, this is an emergency," she said. "I will buy your horse for fifty dollars."

The old man agreed to sell the horse because he thought it wasn't going to last much longer. He said he would drive it to her aunt's house. So the girl jumped on the wagon and drove it herself.

"How did you learn to drive like that?" the man asked.

"I was raised with horses," she said.

They got to her aunt's house and she signed the check over to the man and said, "You may leave now."

"But how will I get home?" the man asked.

"That is your problem," said the girl.

So he started walking.

The girl unhitched the horse and let it into the yard where it started eating grass. The aunt was not very pleased to see a beat-up looking horse in her front yard. But the girl said she would have the horse shipped out to the ranch. She knew her father would approve when he saw it.

On the ranch, the horse soon recovered its strength and turned out to be a beautiful creature. The girl called it Sprite. And it won many races and finally was retired and gave birth to many foals which also won races.

When I finished and read it over, I thought it was pretty good. I could hardly wait for Betsy to get back so I could show it to her. The first of August came at last, and she was home. She rushed over at the first opportunity, and I took her up the ladder and showed her what I had found. She was just as amazed as I thought she would be.

"That's a neat painting," she said. "I saw some like it when we went to Saratoga."

"Saratoga?" I said. "What's there, besides the race track?"

"There's a racing museum," she said. "Maybe we can go again some time and you can go with us."

"I hope you will," I said, "because my family sure isn't going anywhere."

I read Betsy my story and she thought it was great.

"You ought to write more," she said. "How about 'Daughter of Sprite'? Or how about this girl—what's her name?"

I had been thinking of calling her Caroline, but I saw that wouldn't do. "Katherine," I said.

"Okay, how about Katherine coming east with her horse and riding her in one of the big races?"

That seemed like a good idea, so we started in on it. We were having so much fun that we were surprised when Mother drove in and called to me to come help bring in the groceries.

We climbed down the ladder and Betsy got on her bike and rode home.

It was a warm afternoon. Tom came home covered with paint and sweat. He sat on a kitchen stool and drank a can of Coke. I helped put away the food. Mother started making a salad.

Then Dad came in. He had walked from the station and his coat was over his arm and his tie was hanging loose and he looked really beat.

"Take a shower," Mother said, "and I'll fix you a drink."

But Dad flopped down in a chair. "Better have dinner soon," he said. "I've got to go up on the roof and fix some shingles."

"Why do you have to do it tonight?" Mother asked.

"Because it's going to rain and we'll have a leak," Dad said. "I'm afraid we'll need a new roof."

Tom said, "Hey, Dad, I'll go up and put a tarp on the roof and we'll fix it this week-end."

But Dad said no, he wanted to do it right away. So we had dinner and Tom and Dad went out to fix the roof.

It struck me that this new way of life wasn't working too well. What about that horseshoe on the stable that was supposed to bring us good luck? So far it was just bringing trouble. We had moved to the country so we wouldn't have to drive out from the city, so Mother could play tennis and garden, and Dad could sketch and paint, and I could ride a horse.

But Mother and Dad had no time for anything but work. It's true Mother liked her job, and Tom was enjoying painting houses and earning money. And riding after all wasn't too important, I tried to tell myself.

The problem, I decided, was Dad. He was getting more and more tired and even cross, which he never used to be. He was bringing work home from the office and sitting up late and in the morning he could hardly get out of bed.

"What's the matter with Dad?" I asked Mother one evening.

"He's worried about expenses," she said.

"He ought to take a vacation," I said. "We haven't even gone out for a drive in weeks."

"I know," Mother said. "Maybe this house was a mistake. We may not be able to swing it. Tom has one more year of school and then there will be college. That will be a huge expense. I'm going to have to find a better paying job." I could see she was worried.

That night Dad ate in a hurry and got up. "I have some paper work to do," he said.

Mother said, "Oh, Don, can't you take an evening off?"

He said, "No, the man is expecting it in the

morning. Will you please let me make my own decisions?" he added crossly.

At that point, something came over me. I don't know how I had the nerve, because kids aren't supposed to tell their parents what to do. But I decided to say what was on my mind anyhow.

I said, "Dad, you haven't done any painting this summer. That's one of the things we moved out here for. Why don't you stay home and paint for a while?"

They all stared at me as if I had lost my mind.

Dad said, "It's a nice thought, but I've had my vacation."

"Take another," I said. "You need it."

Mother said, "Caroline, don't be fresh." But suddenly she looked at Dad. "You know, it's not a bad idea. Maybe we should think about it. A leave of absence."

"Without pay?" said Dad. "Do you know what our expenses are?"

Then Tom said, "I can get a job. The carpenter offered me one for the rest of the summer. Would that help?"

"Anything you make has to be for college," said Dad. "You people are crazy, I hope you realize that. Besides, I haven't got a studio."

"Oh, is that all?" I said, as a new idea flashed through my mind. "Follow me."

I got up and started for the stable. Dad came too. He probably thought I was really crazy and he had to watch me.

"Where are we going?" he asked. "There's no room in the shop."

"Be patient," I told him, starting up the ladder.

When he saw the attic, he was amazed.

"How come I haven't been up here?" he asked.

"You've been too busy," I said.

He looked all around. "It's got possibilities," he said. "It even has a north light. Pretty hot, though."

"I couldn't get both windows open," I said. "If you can put screens in, and get a fan, it might do. It's mine, but I'll rent it to you."

He laughed, for the first time in a week. "What do you charge?"

"A painting for my room," I said. "Actually, I have the painting, but I can't get it down the ladder."

I pointed to Sprite.

"What's that?" he asked.

"That's my horse Sprite," I said.

He got down on his knees and examined it. Then he wet his finger and rubbed off a little dust and said, "That's a very good painting. How did it get here?"

"I found it here," I said. "It looks like it's always been here. It's too big to go through the hole."

"Very strange," he said. "Whoever owned the house must have rebuilt the opening after they put the stuff in here. Let's see what else is here." We looked at the other pictures.

"Just mediocre things," Dad said. "This is the only good one. I wonder who the artist was."

We looked it over carefully but couldn't find a signature. Just the name of the horse and rider on the back.

I said, "Well, what about the studio? I can't hold it indefinitely."

"I'll let you know," Dad said.

We went back to the house. Dad went to his desk and got to work. Mother and Tom were doing the dishes. I joined them.

"Where have you been?" Mother asked.

"I showed him my attic," I said. "I offered to rent it to him for a studio. But he didn't say yes or no. Why do grownups worry so much?"

"You wait till you have a family to support," Mother said.

That evening, after I went to bed, I heard them talking. They must have come to an agreement, because a few days later Dad said he had talked to his boss, and he would take a month off.

I didn't think a month was enough, but I felt happy anyhow, to think they had actually listened to me. Of course Dad must have had the wish in the back of his mind or it wouldn't have happened.

That weekend he took his painting things over to the stable. He set up his easel and fixed up a table with some boards and boxes. He and Tom put in a couple of electrical outlets so he could have a fan and a good light.

He went to the office for a week, and then he started his month of freedom. He would have most of August and a week of September.

Chapter 4

Every day, Dad was up at the crack of dawn. He worked all day, trying to get as much done as possible.

Of course it meant I didn't have my attic to sit in and write. And also, I was farther away than ever from riding lessons.

But then Betsy had an idea. "Why don't you ask Mrs. Harris if you can help out at the stables?" she said. "Maybe she'd pay you in lessons." Well, it couldn't hurt to ask.

So I rode my bike over and what do you know! She said yes! She let me do jobs like mucking out stalls and leading horses around to cool them off, and in return I got a couple of lessons a week. What happiness!

Once in a while Dad came to Sunnyfield with me and drew landscapes with horses grazing in the fields. He drew riders on their horses, and Mrs. Harris hung some of his sketches in the entry so the kids' mothers could see them. Some of them wanted their pictures done.

Then Mother talked to some of her customers in the flower shop and told Dad that a couple of them would like to have paintings of their houses, so he went to sketch the houses.

Mother said, "You know, I found out I'm good at selling. I could start a business selling paintings, if you produce enough."

But Dad told her sternly, "Now don't get carried away. This is just a leave of absence. When it's over, I go back to work."

He was being realistic. Just the same, we all felt good, the way we did the summer before.

Then something unexpected happened. One day when I got home and went to put my bike away, I heard unusual noises overhead. I went up the ladder and there was Dad moving things around. He had the table in front of the window and was laying Sprite on it.

"What are you doing?" I asked.

"I used to work in a shop, restoring paintings," he said. "I've been studying this one and thinking maybe I can fix it."

"No kidding!" I said. I had never heard about this side of his life before. "You mean you can make it look good again?"

"I'm willing to try," he said. "What do you say? It's your painting."

"What could happen?" I asked.

"Well, it's a gamble," he said. "I have to clean it. The cleaning solution could wash away the color. Or the paint could flake off. We don't know what paint the artist used or how it would react. The canvas looks all right but it's old. It might tear. What do you say? Want to take a chance?"

I said, "Go ahead. Live dangerously."

"Okay," he said. "First we have to get the frame off. Then we take the canvas off the stretcher."

He pulled out the nails that held the frame in place, and lifted it off. Without the frame, the picture looked naked. Then he examined the tacks that held the canvas to the stretcher. They were rusty. Carefully he lifted each tack with a knife blade and a tack lifter. One or two broke off.

The wood of the stretcher was old and dry. There were little pieces of wood in the corners, wedged into slots.

"Those are for tightening the canvas," Dad

said. "That's how old stretchers were made."

He lifted off the canvas. I held my breath, watching him. It looked like an old rag with paint on it. He spread it on newspapers on the table.

"What a relief," he said. "It came off in one piece. I was afraid it might tear. Well, that's enough for now."

And we went down to supper.

"What are you two guys up to?" Mother asked.

"You'll see," Dad said, mixing drinks for them. "It's an experiment."

The next morning, we took the vacuum cleaner up to the attic. "Better get this place as clean as possible," Dad said. "Dust is bad for wet paint." So I cleaned the floor and the walls, and then he vacuumed the picture with a soft brush.

Then he mixed some stuff in a bowl.

"What's that?" I asked.

"Alcohol and castor oil," he said. "Not good to drink."

"Ugh!" I said.

He took a piece of cotton and started sponging the canvas very gently with the mixture.

"The alcohol takes off the dirt and old varnish and the oil keeps it from acting too fast," he explained.

The surface, which was dull and yellowish, began to look fresh. The yellow sky became blue.

"Now we begin to see the real coloring," Dad said.

"I thought it was supposed to be yellow," I said.

"It's the varnish that gets yellow. Then people think all old pictures were painted that way."

As the varnish came off he looked carefully at the piece of cotton. Some chips of paint were coming off. He picked them carefully from the cotton.

"I'll have to repaint," he said. "But it's minimal. And the alcohol's not taking the color off. That's good."

He was mumbling more to himself than to me.

"Why is it good?"

"Sometimes a painting is retouched. Then the alcohol can take off the retouching. And sometimes it can take off the original color. But this is just cleaning off the varnish. Okay, that's enough for today. We'll leave it to dry.

50

Let's hope there aren't any mice to track across it." We went down the ladder.

"I'm going over to clean stalls," I said.

"I'll drive you," he said. "Maybe I'll do some sketching."

I made sandwiches and we took off for Sunnyfield. It was like old times.

After I got through with my chores, Mrs. Harris said, "I'm taking a small class out in a few minutes. The girls are more advanced than you but if you want, you can come with us. You can ride Brownie."

Did I want? What a foolish question!

But after we'd ridden around the ring a few times she said, "Let's do some jumps!"

I'd been over some rails laid on the ground, and even one about a foot high, but the ones set up that day were two feet high or more. Just looking at them was scary. I would have pulled out if Dad hadn't been there with his sketch book.

"Want to try it, Caroline?" Mrs. Harris asked.

I nodded, my throat too dry to speak.

But she was right there beside the first jump as we cantered up to it. When it came my turn and I was a couple of strides away, she spoke to me.

"All right, Caroline. Heels down, get forward a bit, hands on Brownie's neck. Now, up and over!"

Well, Brownie knew what to do, even before I touched him with my heel. It was a wonderful feeling. I wanted to keep on and on, but after a few more jumps, we all dismounted. We walked the horses around a bit and rubbed them down.

When we were leaving, Dad thanked Mrs. Harris for letting him stay.

"Any time," she said. "We like to have a resident artist."

We went off and sat under a tree, and ate our lunch, and Dad showed me his sketches. There I was on Brownie, leaping over the hurdle, with my hair flying out behind.

"Can I have it?" I asked. "It will pay your rent for the attic for this week." Then I sighed. This was so much fun.

"Wouldn't it be nice to be rich!" I said. "And do things like this all the time."

Dad shook his head. "No. If we were really rich, this wouldn't be so special. Besides, I'd have to spend all my time taking care of my investments. Pretty boring, don't you think?"

But there was a slight frown on his face as

he said it. I knew he was worried. "Well, just a little rich," I said.

The next day, he did some more cleaning. This time he went over the horse's body and we could see how shiny and black she really was, like black satin. She stood in a field, with green trees behind her. The jockey's colors were red and blue.

We left the picture to dry. Every day for a week Dad worked on it for a little while. Then he said it was time to put on a lining. He carried an electric hot plate up to the attic, and a battered old double boiler with water in the bottom part.

"Go and get me Mother's iron," he said. I went, wondering what that was for.

When I arrived he had a piece of linen laid out on the table. That was the lining.

He took the double boiler and started mixing some stuff in the top, mumbling to himself, "One third resin, two thirds wax." Then he put the boiler on the hot plate to melt the resin and wax together.

"What are you making?" I asked. "Some kind of pudding?"

"An adhesive," he said. "A kind of glue."

"What's resin?"

"It's like pitch from a pine tree. The wax is beeswax."

He laid the picture face down on some newspapers, and brushed the warm glue over the back of it very carefully. "This will soak in and fasten the chips of paint in place," he said.

Then he laid the lining on top, smoothed it out, plugged in the iron, and began to iron back and forth, slowly.

"Now we'll leave that to cool and hope for the best."

We went down for lunch. When we returned I held my breath as he lifted the canvas with the lining attached, and turned it over.

"Great!" he said with a sigh of relief. The painting was stuck fast to the lining and looked less like an old rag. The only thing was, the writing on the back was covered.

"Don't worry about that," said Dad. "I'll take care of it." I didn't understand, but he was too busy to explain. The canvas had to be put back on the stretcher and fastened with new tacks. Then it was put on the easel. And then came the hardest part—filling the little holes and repainting wherever bits of paint were missing.

It was slow work. Dad had to study the brush strokes and the color, to be sure they would match the original. It took a long time. He could only do a little every day. Then his month was up and he had to go back to the office.

Though it was still warm and sunny, the summer was almost over. Here and there a branch of a tree burst out in flaming red or gold, to remind us that it wouldn't be long until fall.

Mother said I needed to go shopping for new clothes. I didn't want to. "I have no time," I said. "I have plenty of clothes."

But she insisted, and practically had to drag me kicking and screaming. Then she bought me a new blazer, so I felt better.

Then Labor Day came, and the town picnic in the park. Bridgeton has it every year and it's great. Every family brings food and we cook out and then have races and a softball game, and when it gets dark we shoot off fireworks, and sing. It's like being part of a big family.

And the next week school started and I was busier than ever. I met some kids I knew, and some new ones. After school I went to Sunnyfield.

And on weekends Dad was working on Sprite. He worried about the hole in the corner of the canvas.

"If only we could find that missing piece," he said, "I wouldn't have to put in a patch."

But though Betsy and I crawled all over the floor with flashlights, we couldn't find a thing. "Maybe we sucked it up with the vacuum cleaner," I said.

It was raining that day and there wasn't much to do. We went down to my room.

"You know," I said, "if we can't find out about the artist, how about the horse? Do you think it was a real horse?"

"Why not?" Betsy said. "Why would that writing be on the back otherwise?"

"Well, who would know?" I asked. "Who knows about horses?"

"I've got it!" Betsy said. "Why didn't I think of it before? The racing museum. Write them a letter. What can you lose?"

"What's their address? You said they were in Saratoga."

"I think we should have the exact name and address," Betsy said.

We went to the library and found a book all about different museums. We looked under New York, and then under Saratoga, and there it was: "National Museum of Racing, Saratoga Springs, N.Y. 12866." I wrote a letter and copied it on Mother's typewriter:

Dear Sirs:
    I would like to have some information about a horse. I have seen a picture of this horse, whose name was Sprite, with a jockey named O'Brien. Was it a real horse, and can you tell me anything about it? I am doing this for a project. Thank you very much.
Sincerely,
Caroline Keating.

"That's good," Betsy said, approving of my effort. "You didn't tell them you own the picture, or they might say you should bring it up for them to see."

"Yes, and then I would have to explain that I can't get it out of the attic because the hole is too small."

I didn't tell Dad what I had done. I was afraid they might not answer, and he would laugh at me for being childish. I waited.

And then one day a letter came. I was glad I was the first one home to pick up the mail.

I tore open the envelope with trembling

fingers and pulled out some papers. On top was a letter which said:

Dear Miss Keating:
 Thank you for your letter. We are glad to be able to answer your question. Sprite, the filly you inquire about, was well known for many years and is in the Racing Hall of Fame. She raced 180 times, finishing first 60 times; second, 25; and third, 28. She was foaled in 1894 and was known as "Dark Lady."
 We enclose a copy of an article about her from *The Blood-Horse*.

The Blood-Horse was a journal with news about race horses. There were three pages in very fine print, with a photograph of a black mare named Sprite, also called the Dark Lady. It gave her pedigree and a complete history of her life, telling who owned her and where she raced and how much money she won. But it didn't tell anything about who painted her picture.

 Dark Lady, I thought. What a lovely name!
 I phoned Betsy, and she came over and we read the whole article and were so excited that

we forgot it was nearly supper time and I was supposed to put a casserole in the oven.

"I want to be here when you tell your Dad about this," Betsy said.

I said she'd better stay for supper and we went to the kitchen. Mother and Tom came home, and as usual Dad was the last to show.

"Now wash up and sit down. We want you to be sitting down because we have a surprise for you," I said.

Then we produced the letter and the article. His surprise was monumental.

"You little sneaks!" he yelled. "To go and write to them behind my back!" And he laughed and jumped up and hugged us both.

Then Mother, with her good business sense, said, "It's a good thing *they* did it. If you had written, they would have wanted to see the picture."

"Yes, and it's not ready to be seen," Dad said.

"Speaking of which," said Mother, "has it occurred to you that Tom and I haven't seen it yet? Officially, that is."

Tom grinned. "We snuck up the ladder when you weren't here," he said. "I was thinking, Dad, that when you get ready to take that picture out, you'll either have to take the roof off or make a bigger hole in the floor. Why don't we open it up and put in a disappearing staircase?"

Dad said he had no time, but Tom said, "I can do it Sunday. Kevin can help me. I just did one for my boss." Tom was working for the carpenter on Saturdays.

So he ordered lumber and started to saw a big hole in the attic floor. But before he could do that he had to rip out a couple of floor boards. Betsy and I were watching, getting ready to help, when suddenly between two boards I saw something. It looked like a little piece of rag.

"Wait!" I yelled. "Don't move!" And I poked my fingers in between the boards, getting splinters in my hand, and pulled out—you guessed—the missing piece!

"I found it!" I screamed.

"Eureka!" yelled Betsy.

Tom thought we were both crazy, till we showed him that the piece fitted the hole in the picture. But did it have the artist's signature? No, not that we could see. It was disappointing. But at least Dad wouldn't have to put in a patch.

We went to the house and I found a silver

tray that Mother kept wrapped in flannel. I put the piece of canvas in the middle of the tray with a rose from the garden, and when Dad came home I presented it to him with a deep bow.

"Incredible!" he said. "I just don't believe it."

That weekend he cleaned the piece, and we examined it with a magnifying glass.

"Doesn't that look like an *R*?" I asked, pointing to a faint squiggle.

Dad squinted at the scrap of canvas. "You may be right," he said. "And this might be a *T*. Looks as if it was signed with initials. That sometimes happens."

"I think it's an *F*," I said. "Who is F.R.? T.R. would be Theodore Roosevelt, but he didn't paint horses, did he?"

We were sure it was F.R. We looked in the dictionary but there was nothing about an artist with those initials.

The next day I went to the library and found a whole encyclopedia about artists. Only it was in French. The librarian helped me. I was dying to find out that F.R. was somebody really famous.

Frederick Remington! Could it be? When Dad and I were going to museums and galleries, I saw some Remingtons. In my opinion he was about the greatest horse painter who ever lived. But did he paint horses standing still for their portraits? No, most of his horses were in action—leaping over walls or tearing across the desert. If they stood still, they were in a snowstorm with their backs to the wind and their heads drooping. He did paint some race horses, it's true, but they were in action too.

No, it wasn't Remington. I looked further. Rembrandt? Of course not. Rousseau? No. Anyway their first names didn't start with *F*.

Oh, well, what did it matter anyway? Dad was happy because the missing piece had been found. He glued it in place and touched up the torn edges.

The next weekend he worked on the frame, while Tom worked on the staircase. He filled in the chipped places with new plaster, and then gilded it. And at last he and Tom carried the picture down the stairs and stood it on a table in the living room, against the wall.

When I came in from riding, there was my horse, looking so beautiful, I almost cried. She shone as if she had just been polished, with one little white blaze on her forehead.

And at the bottom of the frame was a little

brass plaque engraved with the words *Sprite, O'Brien Up. F.R. 1905.*

So that was what Dad had been thinking of when I asked about the writing on the back, and he said he would take care of it.

For a moment I couldn't talk. Then I whispered, "Dad, she's magnificent. Where shall we hang her?"

He looked a little sad and shook his head.

Mother said, "Caroline, we can't hang her. She's too big for our house. We don't have a wall that's big enough."

I said, "I'll take everything out of my room."

"Besides—" Mother stopped and looked at Dad. He looked at her, and then Tom looked at them both. Suddenly I understood the meaning of all those glances.

"I know," I said. "You want to sell her, but you're afraid I'm going to scream."

"Not quite," said Dad. "We were afraid you might cry, though. Actually, I think it would be possible to sell her. There's a market for sporting pictures, and we do know the horse, thanks to you, even though we don't know the artist. But you would have to make the decision. You found her."

"And you did all that work," I said. There

was a lump in my throat, but I went on. "I think you're right. If you know how to sell her, you should."

"I'm not sure about the best way to do it," Dad said. "I think I'll ask the Brownells. And I wouldn't sell her unless we could get a good price."

I said, "Okay. There's only one thing, though. Can I have her in my room for a while before you send her away? I want to look at her."

"And talk to her, no doubt," said Tom.

My face got red. He'd been listening to me and Betsy chattering away in the attic.

"You get lost," I said rudely and walked off quickly before I could make a fool of myself.

Chapter 5

This put a whole new light on the matter. I had never dreamed of my Dark Lady in terms of money. I didn't like to think of her that way. I loved her, and you can't sell something you love.

On the other hand, I had to admit to myself it was practical. Also, if Dad could restore one old painting and sell it, he could do others.

Betsy and her parents came for dinner. They were very excited about the picture.

Mr. Brownell had some suggestions. "First," he said, "don't talk about it to anybody. I know it's an exciting story, but it's better not to spread it around."

He also knew of several auction houses that might sell it. "I'll find out when there's a good sale," he said. "But one thing you should do right away is insure it."

That surprised Dad, even though he was in

the insurance business. "You think our homeowners' policy won't cover it?" he asked.

"I'd insure it for at least five thousand dollars," said Mr. Brownell. "Even if you never sell it, it's a good painting."

"Caroline would like to keep it," said Mother.

"I would, too," said Betsy. "I wouldn't sell it, not unless I was starving."

As she showed no signs of starving, and neither did I, this was just a figure of speech.

"Can we be excused?" I asked. And Betsy and I each took another slice of pie and departed to my room to feast our eyes on the Dark Lady while we enjoyed the pie.

"What I want," I said, "is to find out about the artist."

"But how can you do that?" said Betsy.

I said, "Maybe we can find out who owned the house before us."

"It would go way back," said Betsy. "The picture is dated 1905. That's back in the olden days."

"Maybe we could ask around," I said. "But not in school. We can't tell why we want to know. That's your father's idea, and he's right. We wouldn't want kids coming up to

see it and talking about it. But I was thinking, isn't there some place where they keep track of who owns houses?"

"The Town Hall," she said.

"You're right. That's where my folks went when we bought the house. They had to clear the title."

So the next day we went down to the Town Hall and talked to the Town Clerk, Mrs. Andrews.

"We're doing a project," I told her. "Could we find out who were the previous owners of our house?"

"Why, I guess you could," she said. "It's public knowledge."

She went to a file and took out a folder.

"Let's see. Your father bought the house in the spring. It had been vacant for a year but before that it belonged to the Beckermans. They lived in it at first but then rented it, I think."

I said, "Who owned it in 1905?"

"I'd have to look it up in some old records."

"Is that a lot of trouble?"

"Well, it is a little," said Mrs. Andrews. "Is this a school project?" It's funny that people think you never want to know something except for school.

"Well, no, but we want to know the history of the house."

I guess Mrs. Andrews wasn't very busy just then. Or she approved of wanting to know history. She went somewhere and came back with a big book.

"Here are the records," she said. "This map shows your section of the village. See, here's your house. Now, who lived in it? It was built in 1890 by a Mr. John Richter. In 1910 the house passed to George Richter. In 1930 it was sold to Simon Beckerman. In 1970 he died and the house went to his daughter, Miss Emma Beckerman. She lived in it for a while, and then rented it to various people. Then she sold it to a real estate firm. Then it was vacant for a year, and then your family bought it."

I made notes of all that information.

"Does that answer your question?"

I said, "In a way. But I still don't know anything about those people."

"What did you want to know?" she asked.

"Was there anybody whose first name started with *F?*"

She laughed. "They didn't put that in the

record. You'd have to ask somebody else."

We thanked her and left. Now what should we do?

"We could go to the library," Betsy said.

"But they'd want to know why we were interested," I objected.

Betsy said, "I wish we could find a telephone book from 1905."

But that was almost eighty years ago. We were pretty sure there weren't any telephone books that old. Could there be any people who were old enough to remember?

I thought of Mrs. Dawson. "Let's ask her. She has lots of good ideas."

Mrs. Dawson was out in the yard watching her baby Jimmy playing in his sandbox.

"Hello, girls," she said. "How nice. What are you doing today?"

I said, "We're doing some research. We thought you could help us."

"Okay, fire away. I'll do my best."

"We want to find out about the people who lived in my house before us."

"What! Those people? They had wild parties and we were always having to call the police."

"No," I said, "not those people. The ones who lived there first."

Mrs. Dawson didn't know. But she said, "Maybe some of the older people would know. I'll ask my mother-in-law. She belongs to the Garden Club and they know everybody."

At that point Jimmy climbed out of his sandbox and came running to throw himself at me. I picked him up and gave him a piggyback ride around the garden.

Mrs. Dawson brought out some cookies and lemonade.

"I'll let you know as soon as I find out anything," she promised, tactfully not asking us any questions. Pretty soon it was time to go home.

Mrs. Dawson reported the next day that her mother-in-law advised consulting the Historical Society. The president was Mrs. Willoughby, and she gave us her telephone number.

I phoned Betsy. "What should I do?" I asked. "You'd better come over."

In half an hour she showed up on her bike. Suddenly I was losing my nerve. After all, wasn't it pretty fresh of two kids to call up the president of the Historical Society?

Probably she would say, "Let me speak to your mother."

Then I would have to explain that my mother didn't know what I was doing.

"What's wrong about it?" Betsy asked. "If it's history, we have a right to know."

I picked up the phone and dialed. I could hear it ringing and I hoped Mrs. Willoughby wouldn't be home. But then a voice said, "Hello?"

I said, "I'm Caroline Keating. Mrs. Dawson said it would be all right to call you."

"Of course," she said. "She told me you might call. You have some questions? Shall we meet at the library? I go there nearly every day."

So that afternoon Betsy and I went to meet Mrs. Willoughby. She wasn't dignified and stately, as I had feared. She was a short, rather plump lady with white hair and a friendly smile, wearing a blue cotton shirtdress.

I explained that I wanted to know about the history of our house and who had lived in it.

"I got the names from the Town Clerk," I said, "but she couldn't tell me anything about the people."

She didn't ask me why I wanted to know. She seemed to think it was a perfectly sensible question. She went to a file cabinet and took out a folder. The label on it said, "Richter House."

We sat down at a table and she opened the folder and picked up a photograph. It was our house. But there were no other houses in sight. There was a white picket fence around the yard. Standing in front of the house were a man and a woman and two little boys. The man, wearing a black suit and hat, looked stern and severe. The woman, also in black, had a worried smile, and the two boys looked solemn and almost scared, as if they weren't used to having their pictures taken.

"It's an interesting story," Mrs. Willoughby said.

This is what she told us. John Richter came to this country from Germany in 1870, when he was about twenty years old. He had a great ambition. In Germany he had worked in a livery stable where horses were boarded or hired. He was very poor. He wanted to have his own house and stable. Then he would be somebody. He worked terribly hard. He married and had two sons. He worked on a farm as well as in livery stables, and did the hardest labor. His wife and boys worked too. At last he saved up enough money to buy land, and he built his own house about 1890. This was all farm land then, and Richter farmed and boarded horses.

He planned for his sons to take over the farm and the stables. The younger son followed orders, but the older son had his own ambitions. He wanted to be an artist.

From his earliest days he was always drawing and sketching. His father said that that was no work for a man. He made him work on the farm, taking care of the horses. But the boy didn't do his work. Instead he was always drawing. His father took his sketches from him and tore them up.

At last he got big enough to run away. He traveled all over, out west, painting the things he saw—mountains, forests, Indians. And he painted horses because he knew them so well, from working with them. Sometimes he sold a picture for a few dollars.

He came back east, but his father was angry and wouldn't see him. He had willed the house and land to the younger son, George.

The older son married, but he couldn't sell his paintings. He had to take odd jobs to support himself and his wife. He worked at a race track taking care of the horses. In his spare time he painted them. Sometimes he sold a picture for forty or fifty dollars.

One day he came back to visit his father and brought him a painting as a gift. But the father wouldn't see him. The son left the painting and went away. He never knew if his father even looked at it.

Then the father died. The younger son died. The house was sold to a man named Simon Beckerman.

One day Franz came back to his native village. He went to the house. The Beckermans welcomed him. They had a young daughter named Emma. Franz got jobs in the village. He made friends with the daughter, drew pictures for her, told her stories. Then he died in 1940.

I interrupted at this point. "Did you say his name was Franz?"

"Yes. The younger son was George."

"How did you find out all this?"

"From Emma Beckerman. He must have told the Beckermans about his life. The Historical Society had a project a few years ago. We went to see many of the old people in the village and asked them about the things they remembered. It's good we did, because some of them have died since then."

"How did Franz sign his paintings?" I asked.

"He just used his initials, F.R.," she said. "He thought he would keep his father from knowing what he was doing."

Mrs. Willoughby turned the pages in the folder. There were some drawings, pictures of a young girl, of horses, of puppies and kittens.

"What happened to Emma?"

"Well, after her parents died she lived in the house by herself. But then she got ill, and did not want to live alone. So she rented the house and moved to a home where she could be taken care of. But there was no one to look after the house, so she sold it to a real estate company. Soon after that, she died. But before she died, she gave us these things and told us all this."

I was stunned. What a story!

I asked, "Could I bring my parents to look at this folder?"

"Of course," Mrs. Willoughby said.

"Thank you a million times," I said. I wanted to tell her about the Dark Lady but I had to ask Dad first.

We went home. We didn't talk much. We

went up to my room and stared at the Dark Lady. It had been in the attic all that time. Did Emma know? No, apparently nobody knew, because the attic was nailed up. Nobody had bothered to open up the ceiling.

That evening, I could hardly eat. I was dying to tell my family. But I had to wait for Betsy. We had decided that she and her parents had to be there too. I was doing the dishes when the phone rang.

Mother answered. I heard her say, "Of course, we'd love it."

"The Brownells are coming over," she told us. She made coffee and got out some cake and some crackers and cheese.

Soon they arrived. Betsy looked ready to explode with excitement.

I said, "Listen, everybody. We have something to tell you. Prepare for a surprise."

Then I told the story of our quest. When I had to stop for breath, Betsy carried on. At last we came to the end. Our audience sat there, spellbound.

Then Dad said, "Kids, you are wonderful. You did a magnificent piece of research. Congratulations and thanks. And now, I have a surprise too. It doesn't detract from yours, it just adds to it."

"What's your surprise?" I asked.

"I just wanted to say that I've spent the last two days in the galleries and libraries looking up F.R. I found out that his paintings are pretty scarce and valuable. The poor guy never knew that they were selling for huge prices. But apparently nobody knew where he came from. He was always a mystery man. And here we have an unknown F.R. I suppose the old man just threw the picture up there and boarded up the attic."

"Why didn't he destroy it?" I wondered.

"I guess he couldn't," Mother said. "After all, he must have felt a little guilty at the way he treated his son. Here he's got a son who is practically a self-taught genius, and he tries to kill his talent."

"It's a crime to kill a talent like that," Mrs. Brownell said.

"That's what I'm saying," said Mother. "And that's why, Don, you must go on cultivating *your* talent. A person is given a talent to be used. He has no right to throw it away."

Mrs. Brownell said, "I've got a little to add to this feast of reason and flow of soul. I've just heard that one of the auction houses is having a sale of nineteenth and early twentieth century paintings in a month. That might be a good time to enter the Dark Lady if you want to."

Chapter 6

We got ready. First we had to be sure we had a good photograph of the Dark Lady. Dad carried her out into the yard where the light was good but a little shaded.

It was a perfect October day. The trees were brilliant, all red and gold. The sky was blue and the leaves came fluttering down, turning as they fell. The air was cool and smelled of fall.

Always before, we used to take a trip out of the city to see the fall colors, but this year we were in the midst of them. It was like living in a golden world. I wished Sprite were a real horse, wandering under the trees.

Dad took a whole roll of pictures, and when they were printed we chose the best one to send with the painting. Then he wrapped the painting in quilts and laid it carefully in the station wagon, and started for the city.

I went up to my room. When I saw the empty place on the wall, I almost cried. Dad had promised to blow up one of the photos for me, but it wouldn't be the same. Well, we had made the decision and there was no going back on it.

When Dad came back, we went to see Mrs. Willoughby, to tell her about the painting. We brought her a copy of the photograph. I would not have blamed her if she had felt hurt because I didn't tell her in the beginning, but I explained that it was a family decision, not my own.

"Of course, I understand," she said. "And besides, the art world knows this artist as F.R. It wouldn't be right suddenly to come out with a story about his identity. But maybe the Historical Society could have the story for its records."

Dad said of course it could, and I promised to write it out.

At last the date came for the auction. It was to be on a Thursday in November. Mother got time off from her job, and Tom and I got excused from school for urgent family business, and we went to New York.

It felt strange to go back to the city, and smell the city air full of exhaust fumes, to wear a skirt and stockings and ride a bus up Madison Avenue, looking at the shop windows full of paintings and antiques and elegant clothes.

We walked into the auction room. It was full of people holding cards with numbers. We got catalogues and looked quickly for Sprite. She was number 130.

There was a reproduction of the photograph, and underneath it said, "F.R., American. *Sprite, O'Brien Up.* Signed with initials F.R. l/l." (This meant lower left.) "22 x 30 inches."

Then it went on: "A copy of an article from *The Blood-Horse* on the black filly Sprite, known as the Dark Lady, accompanies this lot. See illustration."

I didn't think I could live and breathe while a hundred and twenty-nine other paintings were sold. But actually it was quite interesting.

Two men would come out holding a picture and the auctioneer would say, "Lot number one." Or two, or whatever it was. Then he gave the name of the picture and the artist, and somebody would start bidding. I couldn't hear anybody saying anything, except the auctioneer.

"I have one hundred. One twenty-five. Now one-fifty. One seventy-five. Now two hundred."

A woman stood beside him pointing out people who raised their numbered cards to show that they were bidding.

Then it would get more exciting. "Two hundred, two-fifty, now three hundred, now three-fifty, against you, sir. Four hundred, four-fifty, five hundred."

We waited to see how high it would go and finally the auctioneer would say, "Are you all through?" Then he would bang his gavel and say, "Sold for five hundred to number ten." Or twenty. Or whatever.

This went on and on, and it was fun seeing people bid an awful lot for some tiny little picture, or some picture that I thought was just hideous.

And at last I heard, "Lot number 130, *Sprite, O'Brien Up*. By the artist known as F.R. A great amount of interest in this. Documentation is included."

And the two men brought out my Dark Lady and held her up. She looked so beautiful I couldn't stand it. I wanted her back. But I knew this was the last time I would see her, unless she landed in some museum.

The auctioneer said, "Will somebody start?"

And somebody started with $500. I gasped. Then $600. $700. I grabbed Mother's hand and held on tight.

Two people seemed to be having a battle over the Dark Lady. The woman consulted with the auctioneer. Finally, he said, "All through?"

Bang went the gavel. "Sold for —" But I won't tell you what she sold for. You wouldn't believe it.

The men took her away, and they started on the next lot. But we didn't wait. We left, and went and had dinner somewhere. We had a lot to celebrate. Selling the picture meant that Dad had done a really good restoration job. And that meant he could do more. It meant that we had some extra money, so Dad wouldn't have to work overtime, but could spend time painting.

He ordered champagne. I don't know why people have to have champagne to celebrate, except that it costs a lot. I like ginger ale myself. But Tom liked the champagne, and said, "Let's do this oftener."

We talked about what we could do. Mother said, "I'd like us to take a vacation next spring, and go to Europe. I think we ought to go to some great galleries there."

Dad said, "That's just what I want to do. See Stubbs and Landseer at the Tate. And the horses of San Marco in Venice."

I said, "Well, before you spend it all, could I have just a few riding lessons? Now that school is open I don't have so much time for mucking out."

"Yes, you deserve them," Dad said. "You're the one who started all this."

We were all exhausted, so we headed for Grand Central and fell asleep on the train. We got home and staggered up the stairs to bed.

I turned on the light in my room, and nearly fainted. There on the wall was an almost full-sized painting of the Dark Lady.

I screamed: "Dad! Mother! Tom! Come and look!"

They came running, grinning like lunatics. Dad had painted a copy for me. I threw my arms around him and nearly choked him with a hug.

"It's gorgeous!" I gasped.

There's only one thing more to tell. One Saturday, coming home in the twilight from

Sunnyfield, I looked at our house and remembered that photo of it I had seen in the folder in the library. In the picture, the house and the people had looked so sad and solemn. Now it was the same house but different. It was happy.

I could hear Tom in the shop, hammering something. That was where he was happy. He had decided he wanted to work for a while instead of going to college, and learn to build houses.

The kitchen light was on. Mother was making supper. Dad was sitting on a stool talking to her.

I felt sorry for F.R., who never knew what a happy house was. I decided I'd write a story about him, and about the horse in the attic. And maybe some day I'd get a book published, and I'd dedicate it to F.R. And after that I'd buy my own horse, a black filly with a white blaze, and I'd call her

Dark Lady.